GHOSTS

RAINA TELGEMEIER
GHOSTS

WITH COLOR BY BRADEN LAMB

An Imprint of
SCHOLASTIC

All rights reserved. Published by Graphix, an imprint of Scholastic Inc.,
Publishers since 1920. SCHOLASTIC, GRAPHIX, and associated logos are
trademarks and/or registered trademarks of Scholastic Inc.

Library of Congress Cataloging-in-Publication Data

Names: Telgemeier, Raina, author, illustrator.
Title: Ghosts / Raina Telgemeier ; with color by Braden Lamb.
Description: First edition. | New York : Graphix, an imprint of Scholastic, 2016. | © 2016 |
Summary: Catrina and her family have moved to the coast of Northern California for the sake
of her little sister, Maya, who has cystic fibrosis—and Cat is even less happy about the move when
she is told that her new town is inhabited by ghosts, and Maya sets her heart on meeting one.
Identifiers: LCCN 2016004672 | ISBN 9780545540612 (hc) | ISBN 9780545540629 (pb)
Subjects: LCSH: Sisters—Comic books, strips, etc. | Sisters—Juvenile fiction. | Ghosts—Comic books,
strips, etc. | Ghost stories. | Moving, Household—Comic books, strips, etc. | Moving, Household—
Juvenile fiction. | Families—California, Northern—Comic books, strips, etc. | Families—California,
Northern—Juvenile fiction. | California, Northern—Comic books, strips, etc. | California, Northern—
Juvenile fiction. | CYAC: Graphic novels. | Sisters—Fiction. | Ghosts—Fiction. |
Cystic fibrosis—Fiction. | Moving, Household—Fiction. | Family life—Fiction. | California,
Northern—Fiction. Classification: LCC PZ7.7.T45 Gh 2016 | DDC 741.5/973—dc23
LC record available at http://lccn.loc.gov/2016004672

10 9 8 7   17 18 19 20

Printed in China   62
First edition, September 2016
Edited by Cassandra Pelham
Lettering by Jenny Staley
Book design by Phil Falco
Creative Director: David Saylor

FOR SABINA

1

I DON'T THINK SO, CAT. THEY ONLY HAVE THEM DOWN HERE IN SOUTHERN CALIFORNIA.

WHAT ARE WE EVEN GOING TO **EAT** IN OUR NEW TOWN?

WE ARE MOVING. UP NORTH AND TO THE COAST.

DAD GOT A NEW JOB, BUT WE ALL KNOW THE REAL REASON WE'RE GOING.

MY LITTLE SISTER, MAYA. SHE'S NOT A HEALTHY KID.

4

MOM AND DAD ARE DRAGGING US TO **THIS** GLOOMY PLACE, BAHÍA DE LA LUNA, CALIFORNIA.

Bahia de la Luna
Exit ¼ mile

THEY SAY THE SUN ONLY SHINES HERE SIXTY-TWO DAYS OF THE YEAR.

WHEN I HEARD THAT, I'D SAID:

EW, I'D RATHER **DIE!**

WHICH DIDN'T GO OVER VERY WELL.

IT'S FREEZING.
I'M GOING
INSIDE.

THE VEST HELPS LOOSEN THE MUCUS IN HER LUNGS.

LA-A-A-A-A-A-A-A...

CAT'S BOOKS BOX #4

CAT BOOKS BOX #7

HER **SOUL** DOESN'T NEED ANY LOOSENING, THOUGH.

LA-A-A-A   LA-A-A-A

ZZT

MOMMMMMMM??!

15

OOH, A SECRET PATHWAY . . .

MAYA!

WE DON'T KNOW WHAT'S DOWN THERE!

17

SIGH . . .

giggle!

WHHHHHHHHHHHHsssssssssSHHH

MAYBE THIS PATH WILL LEAD US TO --

Rustle

KITTY!!

Rustle

crunch crunch

CAT, LOOK...

THIS STAIRCASE LEADS DOWN TO THE BEACH!

57, 58, 59 -- THERE'S 59 STEPS!

RACE YA!

WAIT!

CLATTER CLOMP

HA HA!

PIFF!

MAYA, THAT WAS DANGEROUS!

Topple

Hee Hee

Wheeze Wheeze

SIT, CAT.

pat pat

BREATHE IT IN . . .

Hffffffff

NOW LET IT OUT.

HWOOOOOOOOOOoooooH

I GUESS YOUR FAVORITE PRINCESS SONG GIVES GOOD ADVICE.

Hee hee!

OH, WE SHOULD TAKE A PICTURE AND SEND IT TO ARI!

click!

TAKE ONE OF ME?

THUMP
THUMP

MAYA?

WHERE ARE YOU?

*COUGH
COUGH
COUGH*

MAYA!

SQUEEZE...

UGH,
SO DUS--

THE GHOST TOUR DOESN'T START UNTIL THREE.

GHOST TOUR?!

DON'T LISTEN TO THIS KID, MAYA. HE'S JUST MESSING WITH US.

BUT, BUT . . .

THERE'S **NO SUCH THING** AS GHOSTS.

SCOOT!

YOU MUST BE NEW IN TOWN, IF THAT'S WHAT YOU BELIEVE.

ONCE YOU'VE ACTUALLY **LIVED** IN BAHÍA DE LA LUNA . . .

YOU'LL CHANGE YOUR MIND.

WELL, NICE KNOWIN' YOU!

GOOD-BYE.

BUT --

GHOSTS AREN'T REAL, MAYA. HE'S JUST TRYING TO SCARE US.

. . . I HOPE!!!

Boop
Boop

freezing!

its sunny back home ☹

did u get new clothes 4 school

maya and i met this weird boy yesterd...

CATRINA! LET'S GO!

WHERE ARE WE GOING, AGAIN?

I TOLD YOU -- THE NEIGHBORS INVITED US OVER FOR DINNER.

AWW, DO I HAFTA GO?

YOU!

YOU.

YOU!

UM, HELLO!

CLATTER

CLINK

ORANGE
NARANJA

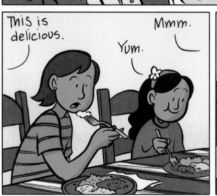

This is delicious.

Yum.

Mmm.

OH **WOW.**

IT'S GOOD, RIGHT? MY MOM MAKES THE BEST TAMALES IN TOWN.

... THEY'RE OKAY, I GUESS.

IS THIS A FAMILY RECIPE, JUANA?

YES, MY MOTHER'S.

GIRLS, I WISH YOU COULD HAVE TASTED YOUR GRANDMA'S TAMALES. YOU WOULD HAVE LOVED THEM.

MY MOTHER PASSED AWAY SHORTLY AFTER CATRINA WAS BORN.

THAT'S SUCH A SHAME.

MAYBE YOU'LL SEE HER ON **DÍA DE LOS MUERTOS!**

IS **EVERYTHING** ABOUT GHOSTS WITH YOU?!

JEEZ!

DIA DAY . . . WHAT?

DAY OF THE DEAD. YOU KNOW, LIKE HALLOWEEN.

NO, GIRLS. NOVEMBER FIRST. IT'S A DAY TO WELCOME BACK THE SPIRITS OF THE LOVED ONES WE'VE LOST. I HAVEN'T CELEBRATED IN YEARS.

OH.

THIS TOWN TAKES IT PRETTY SERIOUSLY.

DO YOU GUYS HAVE A PARADE OR SOMETHING?

HEHEH . . . WE GO **FAR** BEYOND PARADES HERE.

BUT IT'S JUST PRETEND, RIGHT? YOU GUYS DON'T ACTUALLY BELIEVE GHOSTS COME BACK TO VISIT . . . **RIGHT?!**

45

Poke
Poke
jiggle

SO WHAT ARE THE GHOSTS LIKE?

SOME, LIKE MY BROTHER JOSÉ, AREN'T TOO DIFFERENT FROM WHEN THEY WERE ALIVE.

BECAUSE OF THE, UM, **ACCOMMODATING** WEATHER IN THIS TOWN . . .

YOU MEAN THE FOG?

YES. BECAUSE OF THE FOG, THE GHOSTS SEE OUR TOWN AS THE PERFECT PLACE TO HANG OUT.

THANK YOU FOR DINNER, JUANA -- EVERYTHING WAS **DELICIOUS!**

MY PLEASURE.

WHHHHHHHHHHHHHHHHHHHHHHHHHHSSSSSHHHHHH

IT'S JUST WIND AND FOG . . . IT'S JUST WIND AND FOG . . .

"BECAUSE OF THE FOG, THE GHOSTS SEE OUR TOWN AS THE PERFECT PLACE TO HANG OUT."

TCHOOM!

EVERYBODY IN... HURRY... GOOD...

SLAM

PHEW.

READY FOR YOUR NIGHTLY RITUAL, MAYA?

YEAH!

BECAUSE CYSTIC FIBROSIS AFFECTS DIGESTION, MAYA DOESN'T ALWAYS GET ENOUGH NUTRIENTS FROM FOOD.

CAN I SHAKE IT UP TONIGHT, DADDY?

shika
shika
shika
shika
shika
shika
shika
shika

OOP!

SO SHE HAS TO GET THEM ANOTHER WAY.

READY?

YUP.

AWW. MISSING ARI AND YOUR FRIENDS FROM BACK HOME?

YEAH! IT'S JUST . . .

I MEAN, I'M **GLAD** WE MOVED, BECAUSE IT'S BETTER FOR MAYA'S HEALTH . . .

BUT EVERYONE HERE IS TOTALLY OBSESSED WITH GHOSTS! DON'T YOU THINK IT'S WEIRD?!

HOW DO YOU KNOW THERE WEREN'T JUST AS MANY GHOSTS IN OUR OLD TOWN?

YOU JUST NEVER NOTICED THEM.

?!

GOOD NIGHT!!

CLICK!

MOM? HOW COME YOU NEVER TALK ABOUT GRANDMA?

YOUR ABUELA AND I . . . DIDN'T HAVE THE BEST RELATIONSHIP WHEN I WAS GROWING UP.

WHY?

SHE BROUGHT A LOT OF OLD-FASHIONED IDEAS WITH HER WHEN SHE IMMIGRATED FROM MEXICO . . .

BUT I WAS YOUR TYPICAL, STUBBORN AMERICAN TEENAGER.

I WANTED TO DO THINGS THE "MODERN" WAY.

MORNING, CAT.

MMM.

SO, WHEN SHE TRIED TO TEACH ME HOW TO MAKE HER MOTHER'S RECIPES . . .

...I CHOSE TO MICROWAVE FROZEN DINNERS. SHE TRIED TO TEACH ME TO HONOR MY ANCESTORS DURING DÍA DE LOS MUERTOS...

Blink Blink

BUT I WANTED TO TRICK-OR-TREAT WITH MY FRIENDS FOR HALLOWEEN INSTEAD.

BUT TRICK-OR-TREATING IS AWESOME! COULDN'T YOU DO BOTH?

NOT IN HER MIND.

I FEEL BAD ABOUT IT NOW, BUT I NEVER EVEN LEARNED TO SPEAK FLUENT SPANISH.

Scoot

SO I GUESS AFTER YOUR ABUELA DIED... A LOT OF OLD TRADITIONS DIED WITH HER.

CONCHA, CAT?

WHAT'S A CONCHA?

58

JUANA SENT THEM HOME WITH US LAST NIGHT.

HMM... NOT BAD...

KINDA LIKE A DONUT!

YOUR GRANDMA MADE THEM ALL THE TIME WHEN I WAS LITTLE.

CAT, CAN I SEE YOUR PHONE?

WHY?

YOU GONNA PLAY HUNGRY BIRDS OR SOMETHING?

NO, I'M TEXTING CARLOS.

WHAT?! DID YOU GIVE HIM MY NUMBER?!

YEAH, SO I COULD TEXT HIM, DUH!

Later...

KNOCK KNOCK

hi 😊😊😊 u shud come ovr 😊😊😊 lol

MAYA'S HANDIWORK. I'M A BETTER TEXTER THAN **THAT**.

WHAT'RE YOU GUYS UP TO?

CARLOS! WE'RE MAKING AN OFRENDA* FOR OUR ABUELA! COME SEE!!

VERY NICE.

BUT AN OFRENDA NEEDS MORE DECORATING.

OOOH! YEAH!

*AN ALTAR FOR A DECEASED RELATIVE

Peek!

!

DROWNED PIRATES, REVENGE-SEEKING SHIP CAPTAINS . . .

OOOOH! ARE THOSE GUYS PART OF THE GHOST TOUR?

YEAH!

OKAY, THAT'S ENOUGH. NO MORE GHOST TALK.

BUT, CAT!

YEAH, BUT CAT!

WE HAVE TO TAKE THE TOUR! PLEASE, PLEASE, PLEEEEEEEASE?!

NO.

WHY? ARE YOU AFRAID THEY'RE GOING TO "GET" YOU?

NO!!

64

THE NEXT DAY

READY?

PASTRY?

HERE YOU GO, MRS. ALLENDE-DELMAR.

TELL YOUR MOTHER **GRACIAS!**

eye roll

HE SURE IS A NICE BOY, HONEY . . .

NOW, NORMALLY . . .

I CHARGE TWENTY DOLLARS PER PERSON FOR THE TOUR.

OH!

THE ARCADE USED TO BE A BATHHOUSE FOR THE TOWN'S RESIDENTS! EVENTUALLY, GAMES AND AMUSEMENTS WERE ADDED, WHICH SOON BECAME MORE POPULAR THAN THE BATHS.

CAN YOU STILL PLAY THE GAMES?

YOU CAN TRY . . .

ping! ping!

BUT THE GHOSTS HAVE RIGGED THEM SO HUMANS CAN'T WIN.

OH.

TING!

OLD MOVIES **ONLY!** THIS PLACE BURNED DOWN IN 1937 BUT WAS REBUILT TWO YEARS LATER. THEY SAY THE PROJECTIONIST DIED IN THE FIRE . . .

HIS BODY WAS NEVER FOUND, BUT SOMETIMES HIS PHANTOM IMAGE SHOWS UP IN THE FILM PRINTS!

GHOST CRUISE SHIPS (AND GHOST **PIRATE** SHIPS!) TETHER HERE ON DÍA DE LOS MUERTOS.

THE LIGHTHOUSE

A BEACON TO LIGHT THE GHOST SHIPS SAFELY TO PORT.

THE LIGHT DOESN'T ALWAYS WORK... WHICH MEANS **MORE** SHIPWRECKS, WHICH MEANS **MORE** GHOSTS. MWA-HA-HAAAAAA.

THE ALLEY of MURALS

THESE WERE PAINTED IN THE 1960S AND '70S...

MOSTLY, THE PAINTINGS DEPICT REVOLUTIONARY LEADERS FROM MEXICO, BUT THEY --

CARLOS, ARE WE GONNA MEET ANY GHOSTS TODAY?

OH! WELL . . . THEY USUALLY CAN'T BE SEEN THIS EARLY IN THE YEAR, BUT AS WE GET CLOSER TO AUTUMN, YOU'LL NOTICE THEM MORE.

TOLD YOU HE WAS LYING . . .

I'M NOT LYING. GHOSTS REALLY DO HANG OUT HERE.

I CAN PROVE IT.

NO, THAT'S --

OKAY. PROVE IT.

MAYAAAA!

I **HAVE** TO TALK TO A GHOST, CATRINA.

WHAT DO YOU WANT TO ASK IT ABOUT?

Hfffff

I WANT TO KNOW WHAT HAPPENS WHEN YOU DIE.

UH-HUH, AND **I** WANT TO FLY, BUT IT'S NOT LIKE **THAT'S** EVER GOING TO HAPPEN.

DYING ISN'T PRETEND, CAT.

IT'S REAL.

LISTEN . . . IT'S NOT USUALLY PART OF THE TOUR, BUT . . .

I CAN TAKE YOU TO THE MISSION.

IT'S WHERE THE GHOSTS' WORLD AND OURS MOST CLOSELY OVERLAP . . . SO HEADING UP THERE IS OUR BEST CHANCE OF MAKING CONTACT.

LET'S GO.

CAT?

I HAVE NEVER WANTED TWO PEOPLE TO BE MORE WRONG IN MY ENTIRE LIFE . . .

GSHHHH

Shiver

chatter
Chatter

HERE, MAYA . . .
TAKE MY SWEATSHIRT.

WE'RE ALMOST
THERE.

MAYA'S NOT SUPPOSED TO CHASE ANYBODY . . .

...

HER LUNGS CAN'T HANDLE IT!

attempted grab!

successful dodge!

AND NEITHER CAN MINE!

WAIT UP, YOU GUYS!!

76

Whew.

WHHHHHHHHHSSSSSS

Peek

MAYA'S GOING TO BE AMAZED
WHEN I TELL HER I SAW A --

THEN I'M STAYING, TOO.

WHY ARE THEY JUST... SITTING THERE LIKE THAT?

SSSSSSSSS

POP!

DO I DRINK THIS?

NO . . . JUST HOLD IT.

CAT . . . I CAN REALLY SEE HIM!

SO ARE THESE, UM, FRIENDS OF YOURS?

THESE ARE ALL ANCIENT GHOSTS. DEAD FOR CENTURIES.

THEY USUALLY RECOGNIZE ME, BUT THEY CAN BE SLOW TO TRUST NEW PEOPLE.

THEY SEEM TO BE HITTING IT OFF WITH MAYA RIGHT AWAY, THOUGH!

SHE DOES HAVE THAT ABILITY . . .

YEAHHH! CAT, THIS IS AWESOME!!

HA HA!

MAYA! BE CARE--

IT'S MOST LIKELY HER ATTACK WAS BROUGHT ON BY THE COLD. THAT, AND OVEREXERTING HERSELF.

WHHHHHH
SHHHHHH
WHHHHH

CATRINA, WHAT WERE YOU THINKING, TAKING MAYA **HIKING** WITHOUT BRINGING HER MEDICATION?

I'M SORRY! SHE JUST . . . REALLY WANTED TO GO RIGHT THEN, AND I THOUGHT . . .

WE EXPECT MORE FROM YOU, CAT.

I KNOW.

SO I'LL DROP YOU OFF, AND THEN I'M GOING BACK TO THE HOSPITAL TO SPEND THE NIGHT WITH YOUR SISTER.

DADDY WILL BRING THE CAR HOME IN AN HOUR OR SO -- WILL YOU BE OKAY HERE ALONE FOR A LITTLE WHILE?

YEAH.

KNOCK KNOCK

HELLO, CATRINA. WE BROUGHT DINNER.

105

WHY DID I LET THOSE GHOSTS GET SO CLOSE TO HER?

IT'S NOT YOUR FAULT. GHOSTS JUST GET A LITTLE OVERLY EXCITED BY KIDS. THEIR ENERGY IS LIKE A BREATH OF FRESH AIR.

SO YOU **KNEW** THIS WOULD HAPPEN.

NOT EXACTLY! IF YOU SHARE A TINY BIT OF YOUR OWN BREATH . . . SOMETIMES THEY'LL SPEAK TO YOU.

SPEAK TO YOU ABOUT WHAT? COMING TO JOIN THEM?!?

NO! THEY JUST . . . LOOK, I'M SORRY, OKAY? I DIDN'T **KNOW** SHE WAS GOING TO GET HURT!

The schedule card reads:

Name: Allende-Delmo, Catrina
Grade: 6
Student ID: 637792

Per.	Room	Course	Instructor
0	119	HmRm	Vasquez, J.
1	312	21E2 Eng	Mitchell, M.
2	111	21H1 H1S	Nakazawa, K.
3	30	21M5 Ma2	Theodus, T.
4	R	Lunch	--
5	305	21SP Span.	Diaz
6	205	G6 Gym	Lee, J.
7	121	21SC Sci	Garcin, V.

MY NAME'S SEO YOUNG! ARE YOU NEW HERE? I MOVED TO BAHÍA DE LA LUNA FROM IRVINGTON TWO YEARS AGO.

I'M CAT.

I DIDN'T LIKE IT HERE AT FIRST -- TOO MUCH FOG, NOT ENOUGH FROYO -- BUT NOW I LOVE IT! WHAT ABOUT YOU?

HA HA! DEFINITELY NOT ENOUGH FROYO...

THIS IS AMAZING! I'VE BEEN TALKING TO HER FOR THREE MINUTES... AND SHE HASN'T BROUGHT UP GHOSTS ONCE!

SO WHAT DO **YOU** DO FOR FUN IN THIS TOWN?

WELL, THE HARVEST FESTIVAL IS SOON, AND THAT'S PRETTY FUN.

AND . . . HAVE YOU HEARD ABOUT THE MIDNIGHT PARTY ON NOVEMBER FIRST?

YEAH. I'M NOT GOING.

OH, YOU HAVE TO. IT'S GREAT!

LAST YEAR, I MET THE CUTEST BOY I HAVE **EVER** SEEN!

YOU DID?

YES!

TOO BAD HE'S BEEN DEAD FOR OVER A CENTURY . . .

IS THE BREATHING TUBE PERMANENT, MOM?

WE'RE NOT SURE YET, SWEETIE.

YOU KNOW CYSTIC FIBROSIS IS DEGENERATIVE . . . SO, HER LUNGS WILL PROBABLY KEEP GETTING WORSE AS SHE GROWS UP. NOT BETTER.

UH-HUH.

HOWEVER . . . THIS IS MAYA WE'RE TALKING ABOUT.

EVERY TIME SHE HAS A SETBACK, SHE SEEMS TO REBOUND WITH TWICE THE POSITIVE ATTITUDE.

SQUEEZE

IT'S TOO QUIET WHEN YOU'RE SICK.

Tap Tap

AND THEN, THE LEVEL THREE BOSS, C'MON...

DO YOU HAVE THE CHEAT CODE?

I REFUSE TO USE CHEAT CODES, OUT OF PRINCIPLE.

SEO YOUNG, THAT'S THE ONLY WAY TO BEAT IT!

IT CAN'T BE THE **ONLY** WAY, RY...

CAT? YOU OKAY?

LOOKS LIKE SOMEONE'S GOT A CRUSH ON MR. GHOST TOUR...

NO! NO! NO!

Rustle

Rustle

PROBABLY JUST
THAT CAT AGAIN...

I CAN'T LET IT FOLLOW ME HOME TO MAYA!

I KNOW IT'S NOT EXACTLY DOUBLE-BACK BURGER...

THAT'S OKAY, DAD. THANKS.

THEY COULD PROBABLY USE ME AT THE OFFICE TONIGHT -- WE'RE IN CRUNCH MODE THIS WEEK.

WE'LL CLEAN UP.

WILL YOU TAKE OUT THE GARBAGE, CAT?

129

=SQUINT=

SHOOF!!

NOBODY HERE.

YOU HEAR THAT MUSIC, CAT?

UH-HUH.

IT'S PRETTY.

THAT'S WEIRD . . .

IT FEELS LIKE THE SUN IS SHINING.

I MUST STILL BE DREAMING.

CAT!!

IT'S SUNNY! IT'S SUNNY! THE FOG WENT AWAY! IT'S A SUNNY MORNING! GET UP! GET UP! GET UP!!!

Cough cough

141

SHE'S A SUPER FAMOUS **DAY OF THE DEAD** ICON.

REALLY?

YOU SEE HER EVERYWHERE THIS TIME OF YEAR! AND SKELETONS IN GENERAL.

PEOPLE DRESSING UP LIKE THE DEAD HELPS VISITING SPIRITS FEEL LESS . . . AWKWARD AND OUT OF PLACE, YOU KNOW?

YOU WORRY ABOUT GHOSTS FEELING **SELF-CONSCIOUS?!**

IT'S LIKE SHOWING UP AT A PARTY WITHOUT YOUR CLOTHES ON.

EXCEPT THEY'RE SHOWING UP WITHOUT SKIN, EYEBALLS, A DIGESTIVE SYSTEM, FINGERNAILS . . .

CAT!

WHAT'S THE MATTER?

NOTHING! IT'S JUST...

YOU TOLD THEM ABOUT MY BREATHING TUBE, RIGHT?

...

YOU ... YOU TOLD THEM I **EXIST** ... RIGHT?

.....

I'M SORRY I DIDN'T TELL MY FRIENDS ABOUT YOU.

IT WAS SELFISH OF ME, BUT . . .

DING DONG...

...

HERE.

UM! THANKS?

HOW'S MAYA DOING?

SHE GETS A LITTLE BETTER EACH DAY . . .

WELL, TELL HER I SAID HELLO.

CAT? WHO WAS THAT?

CARLOS! HE --

OH!! MY FLOWERS!!

YOUR FLOWERS?

FOR GRANDMA'S OFRENDA. CARLOS PROMISED TO BRING ME SOME MARIGOLDS . . .

THEY'RE THE PERFECT FINISHING TOUCH!

FIRST TRICK-OR-TREATER!

HOWDY.

IS SEO YOUNG HERE?

YOU'RE SUPPOSED TO SAY "TRICK OR TREAT"!!

HA HA ... MAYA, THIS IS SEO YOUNG'S BROTHER, JAE ... WE'RE TAKING HIM OUT TONIGHT. C'MON IN.

THANKS, PARDNER.

HMPH.

THIS ISN'T FAIR.

MAYA, IT'S JUST TOO RISKY TO LET YOU GO OUTSIDE IN THE COLD. YOU KNOW THAT.

I'LL GIVE YOU HALF MY CANDY . . .

THREE-QUARTERS. ALL CHOCOLATE.

OH, FIIIIINE . . .

SO, MRS. ALLENDE-DELMAR!

IT'S COOL IF CAT COMES WITH US TO THE DAY OF THE DEAD PARTY AT MIDNIGHT, RIGHT?!

ErK!

UM, WELL . . . ISN'T THAT A LITTLE PAST YOUR BEDTIMES?

IT'S TRADITION. THE WHOLE **TOWN** WILL BE THERE!

NOT THE **WHOLE** TOWN.

I SUPPOSE IF MOST GROWN-UPS GO, TOO, IT COULD BE OKAY . . .

MEANWHILE

DING DONG

TRICK OR TREAT!

AWW! GREAT COSTUMES!

DING DONG

OH, WAIT, I WAS GOING TO SUGGEST WE AVOID THIS --

TRICK OR TREAT!

HEY, EVERYONE. YOU ALL COMING TO THE PARTY TONIGHT?

OF COURSE!

WOULDN'T MISS IT!

CAT?

IT'S **CATRINA.**

AND **NO.**

HE TOOOTALLY LIKES YOU!!

165

SO YOU'VE CHANGED YOUR TUNE ABOUT GHOSTS, HUH?

WHAT?

THE ALTAR. IN YOUR HOUSE.

OH...

WELL, **THAT'S** JUST FOR MY GRANDMOTHER. MAYA REALLY WANTED TO BUILD HER A LITTLE OFRENDA.

SHE THINKS SHE'LL MEET HER SPIRIT TONIGHT OR SOMETHING.

YEAH, BUT CAT...

YOU OPEN YOUR DOOR TO **ONE** GHOST . . .

YOU'RE BASICALLY INVITING **EVERY** GHOST TO COME INSIDE.

WHAT?! NO!

THAT'S KINDA THE POINT. TO WELCOME WANDERING SPIRITS.

IT'S TRUE. THAT'S WHAT GOOD NEIGHBORS DO.

YOU GUYS, I GOTTA GO!!

BUT WE'LL SEE YOU LATER, RIGHT?

MA'AM.

CAT? IZZAT YOU?

IT'S ME. IS EVERYTHING . . . OKAY HERE?

EVERYTHING'S FINE. WE WERE JUST GETTING READY TO WATCH SCARY MOVIES.

SOUNDS GOOD.

MARCH

CAT. WHY ARE YOU AVOIDING THE PARTY?

I HAVE TO STAY HERE WITH YOU! TO PROTECT YOU FROM . . . STUFF.

WHAT STUFF? GRANDMA?

NO, I'M NOT AFRAID OF GRANDMA'S SPIRIT, EXACTLY . . . MOM'S HERE, SO IF GRANDMA COMES, THEY'LL BOTH BE HAPPY.

SO . . . ?

DEEP BREATH IN . . .

Hfffff fffff fff.....

. . . LET IT OUT.

HWOOooooo..

¡GRACIAS!

¡HOLA!

. . . YOU WILL **NEVER** BE LACKING IN SPIRITS TO CALL YOUR FRIENDS!

SEO YOUNG!

¿CÓMO ESTÁ?

WE'VE MISSED YOU!

HI!

GRANDMA?!

OH MY GOSH! **ABUELA?** IS THAT REALLY YOU?

IT'S ME, CATRINA... UM... ME LLAMO CATRINA.

OH, RIGHT...

HWOOO...

¡GRACIAS, SEÑORITA!

TINK

I HOPE IT'S OKAY IF I JUST SIT HERE WITH YOU.

ESTÁ BIEN. ME GUSTA LA COMPAÑÍA.

SU ESPÍRITU ES BONDADOSO.

HM?

GRACIAS.

CAT!

DO YOU REMEMBER BEING BORN?

NO...

DYING'S THE SAME.

ONE MINUTE, I WAS ME...

THE NEXT MINUTE, I WAS STILL ME, BUT LIKE THIS.

BUT THAT MUST HAVE BEEN TERRIBLE FOR YOUR FAMILY.

ALL I KNOW IS, THEY HAVEN'T FORGOTTEN ME, OR ELSE I WOULDN'T BE HERE, LIKE THIS, TONIGHT!

CATCH!

READY?

READY!

HEYYY! GOOD TO SEE YOU, NEIGHBORS!

MAYA!

SHH . . . MY PARENTS ARE SLEEPING.

GASP!

... WHAT IS IT?

JOSÉ, IF I DIE, CAT WILL BE ALL ALONE. SHE'S TERRIBLE AT MAKING FRIENDS.

OR AT LEAST, SHE USED TO BE ...

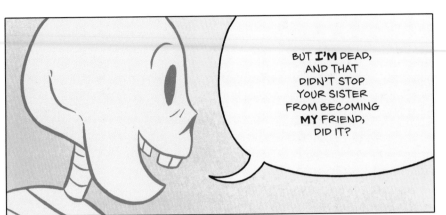

BUT **I'M** DEAD, AND THAT DIDN'T STOP YOUR SISTER FROM BECOMING **MY** FRIEND, DID IT?

I GUESS THAT'S TRUE.

SO YOU THINK I'LL STILL MAKE NEW FRIENDS, TOO?

YOU LOSE CERTAIN THINGS WHEN YOU DIE, BUT NOT EVERYTHING.

AND THERE ARE CERTAIN BENEFITS TO BEING A GHOST!

THERE ARE?

225

229

233

I DON'T SEE ANYTHING . . .

Shrug!

WAIT A SECOND, CAT . . . DO YOU SEE THAT?

THERE'S SOMETHING COMING TOWARD THE HOUSE . . .

MORE TRICK-OR-TREATERS?

NO...

PRRRRRRRR

OH! HA HA!

IT'S THE KITTY! HI, KITTY.

MROW.

SHOULD WE LET IT COME INSI--

DASH!

239

AND SO WE DID.

A FEW NOTES ABOUT
GHOSTS

BAHÍA DE LA LUNA

Bahía de la Luna was inspired by foggy coastal Northern California, where I grew up. I've always had an appreciation for the windswept coastline, the gnarly cypress trees, and especially the seaside town of Half Moon Bay, which is famous for its artichoke fields, pumpkin farms, and cheerful, laid-back Halloween vibe. I wanted Bahía de la Luna to feel like that, and the characters who live there to reflect the laid-back, gnarly, slightly haunted atmosphere.

DÍA DE LOS MUERTOS

Día de los Muertos, or Day of the Dead, is an ancient tradition that is now largely celebrated in Mexico and throughout the world. Instead of mourning the loss of loved ones, Mexican culture chooses to celebrate and honor the dead each year at the beginning of November, building altars (ofrendas) in homes, parks, and cemeteries, and decorating them with flowers, food, photographs, and other personal items. Although Day of the Dead represents the afterlife, there is something undeniably joyous about it!

I was very fortunate to attend San Francisco's annual Day of the Dead celebration during the course of creating this book. Thousands of people came together to dress up, build altars, light candles, and remember their loved ones. It was one of the most beautiful, respectful, and moving experiences I've ever had. Many of the visuals from the celebration scene in *Ghosts* came directly from that night, as I sat, sketched, and observed everything and everyone around me. The process of creating a book is not unlike letting go of the things that haunt your past. Making peace with your ghosts is as profound as the idea of life itself. And at the end of the day, love transcends life and death.

A photo taken of me at San Francisco's annual Day of the Dead celebration, which I attended while working on this book.

CYSTIC FIBROSIS

Cystic fibrosis is a genetic disease that causes thick, sticky mucus to build up in the lungs, making breathing difficult and leading to frequent infections. Some of the treatments Maya endures in this story are the vibrating vest designed to break up the mucus in her lungs (making it easier to cough out); extra nutrition delivered through a port in her belly while she sleeps; and, eventually, a breathing tube to administer more oxygen. Scar tissue can build up in the lungs following infections, reducing the space available for air to pass through. In some cases, CF patients need to undergo lung transplants. While there is no cure, improved treatments for CF have greatly extended the life expectancy of patients. I chose to write about cystic fibrosis because breathing is a huge theme in this story. Ghosts can't breathe, and Maya can't breathe very well herself. Cat has normal lungs, but she is often anxious and sometimes needs to be reminded to stop and breathe deeply. You can learn more about cystic fibrosis at www.cff.org.

SKETCHBOOK

These sketches were done in 2008, eight years before the publication of *Ghosts*! The characters, their story, and this environment have existed in my head for a very long time.

THANK

This book drew a lot of inspiration from my cousin Sabina Castello Collado, whom we lost to cancer when she was thirteen. Sabina was one of the most inspiring kids I ever met: spirited, joyful, and not interested in letting her illness define her or slow her down. She is greatly missed and will never be forgotten.

Sabina's parents, Suzanne and Dioni, and her siblings, Sophia and Adonis, also blew me away with the depth of their love for their daughter and sister. They are incredible people and I wish to thank them for everything they are and everything they do. Special thanks to Sophia for being one of the coolest big sisters I've ever known.

Thanks to Dave Roman and the Cuevas, Roman, Rigores, and Fernandez families for their support. Special thanks to Tammy Diaz Cuevas for talking tamales with me.

The cystic fibrosis community, especially the brave families who posted their stories online, was a constant source of inspiration as well as a great resource for understanding.

My editors, Cassandra Pelham and David Saylor, nurtured this project from the ground up and helped me down the winding path that leads from one ocean to another. I can't think of two better people with whom to wander the windy hillside that is creating graphic novels.

Thanks to Phil Falco, Sheila Marie Everett, Lizette Serrano, Tracy van Straaten, Lori Benton, Ellie Berger, Bess Braswell, Antonio Gonzalez, Caitlin Friedman, Michelle Campbell, Emily Heddleson, and the rest of the incredible team at Scholastic. I love working with all of you.

Braden Lamb deserves an extra-special round of bone-rattling applause for the coloring of my art for this book, translating my notes and reference for the atmosphere of Bahía de la Luna into stunning Technicolor. And muchas gracias to Braden's team of assistants, Shelli Paroline and Rachel Maguire!

Additional thanks to my studio assistants, Alexandra Graudins and Kristen Adam, for providing so much help, never-ending good cheer, and cookies; my wonder agent, Judy Hansen; ace letterer Jenny Staley; Sofia Vasquez-Duran, for talking health and medicine; Jewels Green, for her thoughtful insights on cystic fibrosis; and my friend in all things art, introspection, and skeletons, Ashley Despain.

Thanks to the authors, artists, filmmakers, and photographers who inspired me to think about spirits and magical realism and history and delicious food. Thanks to the librarians, booksellers, teachers, comics community, and everyone who has supported my work so wholeheartedly. Thanks to the state of California, my lifelong muse. Thanks to my family, who don't seem to mind living in the fog; I'll bear it if I have to, as long as you guys are here. Thanks to my friends, who are a continual source of love, support, and ideas. I'd be lost in the dark without them.

Finally, an orange soda toast to my readers, young and old, who are endlessly amazing.

—Raina

BY ANN M. MARTIN
AND RAINA TELGEMEIER

RAINA TELGEMEIER

THE **BABY-SITTERS CLUB**

KRISTY'S GREAT IDEA
BASED ON THE NOVEL BY
ANN M. MARTIN

RAINA TELGEMEIER

THE **BABY-SITTERS CLUB**

THE TRUTH ABOUT STACEY
BASED ON THE NOVEL BY
ANN M. MARTIN

RAINA TELGEMEIER

THE **BABY-SITTERS CLUB**

MARY ANNE SAVES THE DAY
BASED ON THE NOVEL BY
ANN M. MARTIN

RAINA TELGEMEIER

THE **BABY-SITTERS CLUB**

CLAUDIA AND MEAN JANINE
BASED ON THE NOVEL BY
ANN M. MARTIN

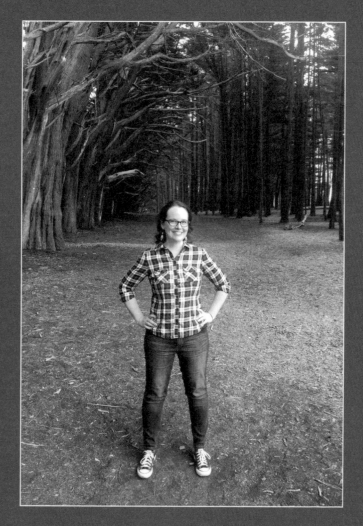

RAINA TELGEMEIER is the #1 *New York Times* bestselling, multiple Eisner Award–winning creator of *Smile* and *Sisters*, which are both graphic memoirs based on her childhood. She is also the creator of *Drama*, which was named a Stonewall Honor Book and was selected for YALSA's Top Ten Great Graphic Novels for Teens. Raina lives in the San Francisco Bay Area. To learn more, visit her online at www.goRaina.com.